TEN little Elvi
gettin' ready to
shine . . .

One made a **comeback**

and then there were **NINE.**

One flew to **Vegas**

and then there were
EIGHT.

EIGHT little Elvi singing about **heaven** . . .

One went to **Graceland**

and then there were SEVEN.

SEVEN
little Elvi

practicing
their **kicks** . . .

One earned a
black belt

KARATE INSTITUTE

and then there were
SIX.

SIX
little Elvi
learning how
to **drive...**

One bought a **Caddy** and then there were **FIVE.**

FIVE little Elvi

struttin' out the **door . . .**

One got his **heart broken**

and then there were

FOUR.

THREE little Elvi

wearing **blue suede shoes** . . .

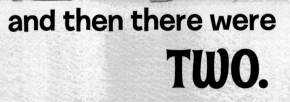

One was **stepped on**

and then there were **TWO.**

TWO little Elvi

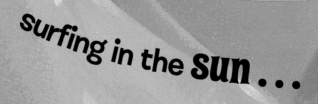

surfing in the sun . . .

One **wiped out** and then there was **ONE.**

ONE little Elvis, sorting through the **mail,**

got invited to a party at the **county jail.**

ONE little Elvis,
feeling lonesome for his **friends,**

went to the party
to see them **again.**

TEN little Elvi

have left the building.

C.Lit PZ 8.3 .H4194 Te 2004
Henson, Laura, 1957-
Ten little Elvi

To Mom

...gall: Thanks for your love and support! –Duffy

To my husband for his patience and support. –Laura

For my mother, Helen Jean Gorissen. Thanks for the poster! And everything. –Dean

Text copyright © 2004 by Laura J. Henson and Duffy Grooms
Illustrations copyright © 2004 by Dean Gorissen

All rights reserved. No part of this book may be reproduced in any form without the written
permission of the publisher, except in the case of brief quotatio...

Tricycle Press
a little division of Ten Speed Press
P.O. Box 7123
Berkeley, California 94707
www.tenspeed.com

Design by Toni Tajima
Typeset in Shag Exotica, Shag Lounge, and Shag Mystery
The illustrations in this book were rendered in acrylic.

Library of Congress Cataloging-in-Publication Data
Henson, Laura, 1957-
    Ten little Elvi / by Laura Henson and Duffy Grooms ; illustratio...
        p. cm.
    Summary: Ten children dress up as little Elvis impersonators i...
    ISBN 1-58246-124-4
    1. Presley, Elvis, 1935-1977--Juvenile fiction. [1. Presley, Elvis,
3. Counting.] I. Grooms, Duffy, 1964- II. Gorissen, Dean, 1961- ill...
    PZ8.3.H4194Te 2004
    [E]--dc22   2004000769

First Tricycle Press printing, 2004
Printed in Singapore

1 2 3 4 5 6 – 07 06 05 04

DATE DUE

JUL 1 7 2009			

#47-0108 Peel Off Pressure Sensitive